P9-BYT-166

Dear Parent:
Your child's love of reading starts here!

Every child learns to read in a different way and at his or her own speed. Some go back and forth between reading levels and read favorite books again and again. Others read through each level in order. You can help your young reader improve and become more confident by encouraging his or her own interests and abilities. From books your child reads with you to the first books he or she reads alone, there are I Can Read Books for every stage of reading:

SHARED READING
Basic language, word repetition, and whimsical illustrations, ideal for sharing with your emergent reader

BEGINNING READING
Short sentences, familiar words, and simple concepts for children eager to read on their own

READING WITH HELP
Engaging stories, longer sentences, and language play for developing readers

READING ALONE
Complex plots, challenging vocabulary, and high-interest topics for the independent reader

ADVANCED READING
Short paragraphs, chapters, and exciting themes for the perfect bridge to chapter books

I Can Read Books have introduced children to the joy of reading since 1957. Featuring award-winning authors and illustrators and a fabulous cast of beloved characters, I Can Read Books set the standard for beginning readers.

A lifetime of discovery begins with the magical words **"I Can Read!"**

Visit www.icanread.com for information on enriching your child's reading experience.

HARP35008

www.harpercollinschildrens.com

Library of Congress Control Number: 2015950815
ISBN 978-0-06-236085-4

Book design by Victor Joseph Ochoa

16 17 18 19 20 SCP 10 9 8 7 6 5 4 3 2 1
❖
First Edition

by Donald Lemke

pictures by Patrick Spaziante

Superman created by Jerry Siegel and Joe Shuster
By special arrangement with the Jerry Siegel family.

HARPER
An Imprint of HarperCollinsPublishers

CLARK KENT

Clark Kent is a reporter at the *Daily Planet* newspaper. He is secretly Superman.

SUPERMAN

Superman, also known as the Man of Steel, has many amazing superpowers. Magic is one of his only weaknesses.

LOIS LANE

Lois Lane is a reporter at the *Daily Planet* newspaper. She works with Clark Kent.

THE *DAILY PLANET*

The *Daily Planet* is the largest newspaper in the city of Metropolis.

MR. MXYZPTLK

Mr. Mxyzptlk (pronounced Mix-yez-pittel-ik) is a magical man from the 5th Dimension. He loves to annoy Superman with his pranks.

Inside the Daily Planet Building,
Lois Lane typed a headline:
"Superman Saves the Day (Again)."
Fellow newspaper reporter
Clark Kent peered over her shoulder.
"Isn't that your fourth Superman
story this week?" he asked.
"Have any better ideas, Clark?"
Lois replied with a smirk.

DAILY PLANET
SUPERMAN SAVES THE DAY (AGAIN)

Ka-boom!

A crack of thunder shook

the Daily Planet Building.

Lois and Clark ran to the window.

The sky above Metropolis blackened.

On the street stood a tiny man
wearing an orange suit and hat.
"Who's that?" Lois wondered aloud.
She turned toward Clark,
but he was nowhere to be found.

Out of sight, Clark quickly shed
his glasses, tie, and suit.
A red-and-blue uniform hid beneath.
Faster than lightning, he flew out
of the building as . . . Superman!

The Man of Steel had faced this pest from the 5th Dimension before. The pesky prankster loved to annoy Superman with his magical powers. The hero sighed. “Mr. Mxyzptlk.”

"What are you doing here, Mxyzptlk?"
asked the Man of Steel.
"You've gotten a lot of attention
lately," Mxyzptlk explained.
"What better way to bother you
than stealing some of that thunder!"
Mxyzptlk lifted a bag toward the sky.
The clouds overhead swirled
into a giant tornado,
then funneled into the sack.

"This should make tomorrow's headlines," said Mr. Mxyzptlk. "Or at least the weather page!" The pesky pest tossed the sack toward the Daily Planet Building.

Fwoosh! Superman rocketed toward the bag at super-speed. He caught the sack in midair and wrapped it in his ultrastrong cape.

Ka-blam! The bag exploded like a thousand thunderstorms. The ground shook beneath Superman's feet and the wind swirled around his cape.

The wind whipped up an old

Daily Planet newspaper.

It floated into Mxyzptlk's hands.

The headline read:

"Superman, Person of the Year!"

"These stories are a bunch
of hot air!" shouted Mxyzptlk.
He twirled his hand at the
Daily Planet Building.
The building's rooftop globe
inflated like a hot-air balloon.
It floated into the sky,
lifting the building beneath it.
"Tee-hee!" Mxyzptlk laughed.

“Now that’s what I call
a *sky*scraper!” said Mxyzptlk as
the building reached the clouds.
Superman soared into the sky.
The hero grabbed the building
and pulled with his super-strength.
Superman couldn’t hold on for long.
He was unable to fight
Mr. Mxyzptlk’s magical powers.

The Man of Steel thought fast.
He released the building and
flew toward the balloon.
"Time to bring this pest
down to Earth," thought Superman.
The super hero took a deep breath.
Fwoosh! He released a blast
of freeze breath at the globe.

The hot air inside the
globe quickly cooled.
It deflated like a leaky basketball.
The building slowly dropped back
to the ground with a *thud*!

Then Superman molded the building's
cracked steel and bricks
back together with his heat vision.
A crowd cheered for the super hero.

"News flash," said Mxyzptlk.
"I won't stop until everyone
knows my name!"
Only one thing could send the imp
back to the 5th Dimension.
Superman had to trick Mxyzptlk
into saying his name backward.
The super hero zoomed
into the Daily Planet Building.

Superman returned moments later.
He fought off Mxyzptlk's pranks
throughout the night.
At sunrise, a truck arrived with
the day's *Daily Planet* newspapers.
Superman quickly grabbed a copy.
"Look!" he told Mr. Mxyzptlk,
handing the pest a paper.
"You made the front page!"
"Really?" Mxyzptlk squealed.

★★★★ City Extra
NEWSSTAND
DAILY PLANET

Mxyzptlk grinned at his picture.

Then he spotted the headline:

"Mr. Kltpzyxm Gets Tricked!"

The pest looked puzzled.

"Who's Mr. Kltpzyxm?" he began, before realizing what he had said. Superman smiled as Mxyzptlk disappeared to the 5th Dimension. Metropolis was quiet once again.

Inside the Daily Planet Building,
Lois struggled for her next headline.
"Got any more brilliant
story ideas, Clark?" she asked.
"Sometimes, Lois," Clark told her,
"no news is good news."